The
Three Royal
Children
and the
Purrflyer
Problem

Angela Castillo

FAYETTE
PRESS

To all the awkward cousins.

1

Cousin Adelide

Prince Torrin adjusted the collar of his super-scratchy royal cape and scrunched down in an upholstered chair in the royal receiving room of the castle. He hated wearing his best cape, he'd much rather wear his comfortable, lighter every day one. But today was special, so his parents had insisted he wear his nicest clothes.

"I wish I could take off these shoes and throw them in the moat," he moaned to his brother, Prince Jude, who was thirteen, and his eight-year-old sister, Princess Celeste. "Why do we have to dress fancy for Cousin

Adelide, anyway? She's eleven years old, like me. She doesn't care."

"Mama said we should always look our best for company." Princess Celeste smoothed the skirt of her pink party dress. "At least your clothes don't have lace on them. Lace feels like spiderwebs crawling down your arm." She elbowed him lightly. "Stop fidgeting, you're making me itch more."

"Don't elbow me." Prince Torrin folded his arms and scowled.

Prince Jude glanced up from the book he was reading and frowned. "Behave, you two. We don't want Cousin Adelide to think we're vagrants." (Vagrant is a royal word for people who aren't civilized).

Celeste's coppery eyes widened. "She won't think that. She's going to love us. We'll have wonderful fun every day she's here. She and I will go on pony rides and tell stories and share secrets." She hugged herself. "Oh, it will be so nice to have a girl to play with!"

"She's not going to do that," Torrin protested. *Why do sisters have to ruin everything?* "She's my age, you know. We're going to start a secret club and write a secret code. And maybe you can come, sometimes. If you give me your best yo-yo. Otherwise she's not going to want to play with a baby like you."

"What!" Celeste rose and stomped her foot, hands clenched at her sides. "Torrin, you're just a great big GROWLIE!"

"That's it." Jude slammed his book shut and glared at his brother and sister. "You're both being ridiculous. We need to let Cousin Adelide decide what she wants to do, and who she wants to play with. It's bad manners to expect her to do any specific thing."

Celeste slouched back in her chair, twisting a light brown curl around her finger. "You're right. We wouldn't want someone else telling us what to do, would we?"

"I'd like to see them try," Torrin muttered.

The royal heralds sounded the trumpets at the gates, the grand fanfare only played to announce special visitors. Torrin could see them in his head, all red-faced and sweaty, blowing on their golden instruments with eyes closed and cheeks puffed out. He was glad he hadn't been born a herald. *Even though that might be less boring than being a royal child.* But Cousin Adelide was coming. He shifted in his seat. No matter how much Jude tried to tell him otherwise, Torrin was convinced she would be his friend. And his friend alone.

The king strode into the waiting room, his long splendid cape swirling behind him. He too was dressed in company clothes. His smile curled beneath his graying beard as he saw the children. "You're all dressed very nicely today. Now remember, your cousin doesn't have any brothers or sisters, so it may take a bit of time for her to get used to you."

"Yes, Papa," Torrin said along with his siblings. *Of course Cousin Adelide will get used to us. We'll be the most amazing friends she's ever had. At least, I will. I'll have to make sure Celeste and Jude don't bother her too much. They can be annoying sometimes.*

"Good." The king moved towards the door. "She should be stepping out of the carriage now, so let's all meet her together, shall we? Your mother is already outside."

The three children followed their father through the front door, past the heralds who still appeared a bit frazzled from blowing the trumpets so much.

Their mother, the Queen, stood in the center of the courtyard talking to a person.

For a moment, Torrin wondered if she was a girl or an older woman, like his mother. Her hair was arranged in a pile of curls on her head. Her dress flared out so far out from her knees he couldn't figure out how she'd have fit in the carriage. "Froofy," he muttered. *But maybe her parents made her dress nice for the trip. Maybe she didn't have a choice.*

The Queen turned, her starry blue eyes twinkling as they met Torrin's. "Come, children, meet your cousin."

Celeste stepped up first, holding out her hand. "Hello, Adelide. We're so glad you've come to visit. I'm Celeste."

Adelide stretched out a slender gloved hand. "Charmed, I'm sure," she said in a bored voice. She glanced at Jude and Torrin and gave them a little frown.

A feeling hit the pit of Torrin's stomach. Have you ever opened a present that seemed great from the outside, with shiny gift wrap and a big, fancy bow, only to find out it was a package of socks? That's how Torrin felt. All the dreams he'd had about Adelide being his best friend swirled right out of his head like water down a drain.

He swallowed the last of his hope and held out his hand. "Welcome, Cousin Adelide. I'm Torrin."

Cousin Adelide wrinkled her pert, little nose that had a dusting of freckles. "I see. Hello, Torrin." She grasped the very ends of his fingertips and gave them a tiny shake. She did the same for Jude when he introduced himself.

The Queen raised an eyebrow. "Two days is a long way to journey by carriage, my dear, Adelide. Why don't you come inside and I'll have the children show you to your room."

Adelide gasped. "The children? Don't you have servants for that sort of thing?"

"Yes, we do," said the King. "But I think Torrin, Jude and Celeste would like to be your guides. They've been very excited about you coming."

"Well then." Adelide shrugged her shoulders. "So long as my things are brought in quickly." She clapped her gloved hands, which was a ridiculous gesture because they made no sound. "Coachman, unload my trunks immediately."

"Yes, your Grace." The coachman climbed down from the top of the carriage, a difficult task since he was short and round, almost like a pumpkin. He mopped his bald head with a cloth and went to the back of the carriage.

The King nodded to a few of the heralds and they swooped in to help.

Torrin counted. *5 . . . 6 . . . 7 gigantic trunks? The poor horses!*

Adelide swept her train over her arm and drifted to the children with mincing steps. "You may take me to my room."

The three children led the way, with Cousin Adelide following and the four heralds huffing and puffing behind, with two of the trunks between them.

The Queen had asked Lady Gertle, the children's governess, to oversee preparing the best guest room for Adelide. Though all the rooms in the palace were magnificent, this was the biggest one, with the nicest bed and the plumpest pillows.

As they entered the castle doors, Princess Adelide glanced about the room and gave a sniff. "Well, I must say, your castle is grand. Better than the King of Drawmoore, but not quite as nice as my Papa's, of course."

Torrin gritted his teeth. Ahead of him, Celeste bit her lip. It was rude to comment on castle size, but apparently manners didn't apply to Adelide.

In the grand hall, Jude opened a door to the left and gestured to the group. "Come on, your room is this way. Mama thought you'd like to stay at the front of the castle because it has the best view."

"Probably the most prone to drafts," said Adelide, but she followed him anyway.

The flight of stairs was short, and soon they reached the nicest guest room. Princess Celeste knocked, then opened the door.

Two maids were fluffing the pillows on the bed, while Lady Gertle watched them, hands on her hips.

Lady Gertle turned, her hat, which looked like a small puppet stage, perfectly balanced on her head. "Children, what is the meaning of this?"

Jude waved towards Adelide. "She's here, Lady Gertle."

Cousin Adelide swept Lady Gertle a curtsy. "Are you the one responsible for preparing my room? It's lovely."

Lady Gertle's stern features softened, and she almost smiled. "Yes, child. Yes, I am. And aren't you sweet? What a lovely dress."

Jude, Torrin and Celeste stared at the old woman and the young girl.

"I've never seen Lady Gertle smile before, have you?" Torrin whispered to Jude.

Jude shrugged.

Adelide's head snapped forward. "Whispering is unbecoming to young royals," she said.

"Extremely unbecoming!" Lady Gertle turned to Celeste, Torrin and Jude. "You three leave this room and let your poor cousin rest. She is obviously a proper young lady and she's had a long trip. She doesn't need to be bothered by you rebel-rousers."

Adelide sank into a cushioned chair and fanned herself. "Yes, I need my rest, cousins. I'll see you all at dinner."

They're two peas in a pod. Adelide will probably tattle all the time. Torrin's heart sank even lower.

2

Meeting with

Aunt Maggie

"And at dinner, she told Celeste she shouldn't be allowed to eat with us because she rested her elbow on the table," Jude told Aunt Maggie.

The three children were sitting in their usual spots on the floor in Aunt Maggie's tower room.

Aunt Maggie presided in her leather armchair, with Lester, the talking bat, perched beside her.

"I didn't even rest my elbow on the table," said Celeste. "It was the part of my arm just above my elbow.

And I can't help it that I have shorter arms and was trying to reach the butter. Torrin should have passed it closer." She glared at Torrin.

Torrin would usually give a sharp retort, but tonight he didn't have the heart. He crumbled the cookie Aunt Maggie had given him into bits and dropped them into his tea, where they made little splashes.

"Well, I'm sure you'll all adjust." Aunt Maggie stirred her tea with a tiny silver spoon. "At any rate, you should have invited her to come with you. She's my niece too . . . at least, my great-great-great something niece. And it's not polite to talk about people behind their backs."

Torrin slouched against his cushion. He'd expected Aunt Maggie to sympathize with them, not be on cousin Adelide's side.

Aunt Maggie continued, "She probably hasn't figured out how to be friends with you. After all, she doesn't have any siblings." She smiled. "Be kind, she'll come around."

"Okay, we'll try." Jude's eyebrows knitted together like two caterpillars shaking hands.

"Anyway," Aunt Maggie said briskly, "I'm glad you're here. I was about to send Lester down with a message, and he's just woken up, so he wasn't quite ready to fly anywhere. We've received word from Krispin Kingdom. There has been a royal emergency and the Purrflyer King needs our help."

"The Purrflyers?" Celeste tilted her head. "Who are the Purrflyers?"

"Cats that fly," said Lester. He yawned and covered his mouth with a wing. "Very dangerous for bats. Smaller ones anyways. I'd give them a run for their money if they tried to catch me."

"Cats that fly?" Jude scratched his chin. "I'd say there's no such thing, but I know better after visiting Rellyland."

"Once you've seen a green pony you can believe anything," said Torrin.

"We shall leave tomorrow afternoon." Aunt Maggie rose from her chair. "This time we'll be travelling to Krispinland. Preparations need to be made, so I'll let you children go downstairs, tell your parents and pack. I'll be spending the evening modifying the Windlesoar so it can carry four children instead of three. And Lester of course." She raised an eyebrow. "Torrin would you say Cousin Adelide is about your size and weight?"

Torrin gasped. "You mean you want her to come with us?"

"Of course," said Aunt Maggie. "We'd be mean to leave her behind all by herself. She came to visit you. Besides, don't you think she would enjoy coming on an adventure with us?"

The children looked at each other in horror.

Finally, Jude spoke. "You're right, Aunt Maggie, we should invite her to come. And we will." He pushed himself up off the floor. "Celeste and Torrin we should go get ready."

Torrin stalked down the stairs after Jude and Celeste, his feet scattering clouds of dust with every stomp. Finally he burst out. "Jude, are you really going to ask Cousin Adelide to come with us? She's awful! She'll ruin the whole trip!"

Jude turned, with the annoying patient smile on his face Torrin hated. "Relax, little brother. Do you think Cousin Adelide is really going to want to go with us?

She'll wrinkle her dress in the Windlesoar's baskets. Not to mention she'll get her shoes all muddy in the swamp. There's no way she'll want to go."

"Jude, you're a genius." Celeste beamed.

"Of course I'll go." Cousin Adelide pulled a silken handkerchief from her pocket wiped a smudge from Celeste's cheek. "Why wouldn't I want to travel with the Duchess Margarite? After all, she's family."

The children were outside in the garden sitting at a little round outdoor table on the terrace. Hedges of honeysuckle surrounded them, filling the air with a heavy sweet scent. The sun was dipping below the forest to the west of the palace.

Pink spots deepened on Jude's cheeks. "Didn't you hear what we said? We'll be riding in a flying machine. Through the air."

"We'll be camping in the woods. With snakes. And maybe growlies," said Torrin. "You probably never heard of a growlie, but they're bad."

"We get all muddy," put in Celeste. "I ruined my favorite scarf when it got torn in a bramble."

"Royals must be willing to endure some hardships." Adelide selected a cake from the platter beside her.

"Hardships?" Torrin stared at Adelide's crisply ironed dress.

"Why, yes." Adelide patted her lips with her kerchief. "We have a duty to oversee the surrounding kingdoms. Especially when we happen to be next in line for the throne. Of course, you and Celeste wouldn't know anything about that." She stared pointedly at Celeste and Torrin. "But Jude, you do. We have a great responsibility. Why, I've already visited a dozen of the kingdoms that surround my father's. How many kingdoms have you visited, Jude?"

"Well." Jude's face reddened even more. "Counting our kingdom. Um, two."

Adelide's lips puckered as though she'd eaten a sour lemon. "Oh. Surely your parents know the importance of broadening your horizons! I suppose that's what the Duchess is trying to do, help you learn your duty as a royal."

Torrin rested his chin in his hands. Leave it to ol' Adelide to make adventures with Aunt Maggie seem dull and boring. Until this moment he wouldn't have believed it possible, but there it was.

"I have a few things to pack before I go to sleep. We need all our survival stuff," he said in the most adult voice he could muster.

Celeste hopped from her seat. "I need things too."

The two of them left poor Jude with Adelide. As soon as they got through the door where they couldn't be seen from the garden, Torrin and Celeste raced up the stairs to Torrin's room. They leaned against the wall, gasping for breath.

"I–can't–believe this," said Celeste between breaths. "Why would anyone so uppity as Cousin Adelide want to come along with us. Jude was so sure she'd want to stay behind."

"I know." Torrin slapped his hand against the castle's stone wall. "There's nothing we can do. We'll have to endure. I won't stay behind, Cousin Adelide or not."

"Me either." Celeste folded her arms. "We'd better get packed."

3

Windlesoar's Flight

Lines of light flickered across Cousin Adelide's face where she sat across from Torrin in the Windlesoar's basket. She stared straight ahead, a little lace cap perched on her carefully arranged curls, a picture of perfect composure.

Torrin had expected her to shriek, scream and beg to be taken back when the Windlesoar rose into the air, but she did nothing of the sort, only blinked rapidly the instant they left the ramp from the roof of the castle.

Perhaps her hands, which were folded in her lap, clenched a bit tighter, but it was hard to tell because she still wore the long white gloves she never seemed to go without.

I wonder if she wears them to bed. I suppose Celeste could tell me after tonight. The last time they'd gone on an adventure with Aunt Maggie the children had camped in two separate tents, one for the boys and one for the girls. The thought of camping made Torrin's heart race a little faster. He'd loved sleeping outside. They'd cooked sausages by the fire and seen amazing creatures that didn't exist anywhere else but Rellyland. *I wonder if they have glowmies in Krispinland?* He closed his eyes and settled back against the basket's side. *I'm not going to worry about Cousin Adelide anymore. I'm going to have a good time on this adventure. Poo to her.*

"You shouldn't slouch." Adelide's haughty voice cut through his thoughts. "It's unbecoming to a young royal."

Torrin opened his eyes and glared at her. *Shall I slap you in the face? Would that be unbecoming to a young royal?* But of course he knew better than to say this. Instead he glowered and kept silent.

A murmuring began to come from under the jaunty hat, and Torrin realized Adelide was reciting a poem under her breath. The part he could hear was about some prince who went to help some king fix the roof of his castle. It had to be the most boring poem Torrin had ever heard in his life. Tempted to cover his ears, he instead hummed his favorite battle song, taught to him by the Captain of the Guard. It was a rollicking ditty with ten verses, and he might have hummed louder than he meant to.

Adelide stuck her tongue out at him.

That can't possibly be becoming for a young royal.

Torrin hummed louder. In turn, Adelide spoke the words of her poem louder. Soon they were shouting at each other at the top of their lungs. Adelide's face grew red and Torrin's throat hurt.

After a few minutes of this, they both quieted down and went back to glaring at each other.

Usually, Torrin loved riding in the Windlesoar. But before he'd always ridden with Celeste. Even though his sister could be annoying, as most sisters are, she was certainly a more enjoyable travelling companion than Adelide. He longed to be in the other basket where Jude and Celeste could slouch to their hearts' delight without being corrected. Sipping water from his canteen, he wished for a cup of his mother's honey tea she always gave him when his throat ached.

At long last, he could feel the basket dipping, further and further down, until it landed with a few skidding bumps, then came to a stop.

Jude and Celeste jumped out of their basket with huge grins on their faces.

Torrin moved rather stiffly, his back aching from sitting so straight. But he soon forgot about this as he gazed at the land surrounding them.

Aunt Maggie stretched out her arms. "Children, I present to you, the outer border of Krispinland."

When Torrin had visited Rellyland with Aunt Maggie on their last adventure, he'd felt as though there could never be another place more amazing or magical. But he'd been wrong.

Trees surrounded them, if they were trees. At least, they were tall like trees, and each grew from one tall stalk, with branches on the top. But the trunks were covered by little round, shiny things that sparkled in the waning sun, almost like marbles. And at the ends of the branches, instead of leaves, feathery fronds of dark purple waved gracefully in the breeze.

"Hewhover trees." Aunt Maggie strolled to the front of the Windlesoar, where something dark and leathery, rather like an old, folded umbrella, hung. "Lester, wake up. We've landed and I could use your help."

Two wings stretched out and Lester's face peeped from between them. "Please. What do you need that couldn't possibly wait until a more reasonable hour?"

"Come on, Lester," Aunt Maggie coaxed. "We have an extra passenger this time and you know I couldn't pack as many sleeping supplies. Fly up like a good bat and gather some of those hewhover feathers for us so I can get the beds arranged."

"Awww." Lester yawned. "Why can't humans sleep by hanging from trees like normal folks?" But he flew to the nearest tree. In a moment, long, feathery limbs began to float down to the ground.

Celeste selected one and ran her finger through the fringes. "It's soft as a kitten!"

"We're sleeping on those?" Adelide's eyebrows shot up. "Out in the open?"

"Of course not, we have tents." Jude marched over to one of the travelling baskets and began to pull out bags and parcels. "We all help to get ready."

"Yeah, we have a tent," Torrin said quietly, so no one could hear but Adelide. "But it's not really safe. A growlie could claw through it in one swipe."

Adelide's eyes widened a tiny bit more, but then she tilted her chin another notch. "I'm sure Duchess Margarite would never put us in extreme danger. Besides, we're royals. We can handle ourselves."

Torrin agreed with the last part of the statement, but he would have rather faced a Growlie in the dead of night then admitted it to Adelide.

Aunt Maggie set down the bag she'd been lugging and put an arm around Adelide, her colorful shawl billowing about her shoulders as usual. "I'm glad you two are having a nice conversation, but would you please come and help prepare camp?"

"Of course, your Grace," said Adelide.

"Please call me Aunt Maggie."

"Common nicknames are unbecoming to royals," said Adelide.

Jude's mouth dropped open.

Torrin expected Aunt Maggie to get mad, but she just gave Adelide a gentle hug. "We don't deal with formality out here in the woods. However, when we get to the Purrflyer's castle we will definitely follow your lead. My court etiquette is a bit rusty."

The children worked together to get the tents pitched and wood gathered for a campfire. Besides the unusual trees, they continued to find interesting plants and creatures, different even from the ones they'd seen in Rellyland.

As he was gathering firewood, Torrin found a circle of what appeared to be ruby red mushrooms, but with bright shining gems instead of mushroom tops. When he touched one, it jumped out of the ground. A little face popped out from beneath its red cap and gave him an indignant glare before the creature scampered away. The other mushroom-things also sprang up and ran after their companion.

Aunt Maggie checked over his shoulder. "Blunderbugs. Watch where you step, they're everywhere. Won't hurt anyone, but strangers give them fits."

"Torrin, Jude, Adelide, come quick," Celeste shouted from the stream, where she was filling their canteens with water.

The boys hurried to her while Adelide took her normal mincing steps.

"Look." Celeste pointed to a clump of creamy white flowers with floppy petals.

Torrin folded his arms. "They seem like normal flowers to me."

Celeste shook her head. "Watch."

The center of one of the flowers furled open, and suddenly, a tinkling tune poured forth. The surrounding flowers joined in, playing together in perfect harmony.

Torrin darted a glance at Adelide. A tiny twinkle appeared in her eyes.

As quickly as they'd started, the flowers folded together, and the song stopped.

"Pretty neat," said Jude.

Aunt Maggie called the children to dinner and they sat around the fire, enjoying the simple meal of roast beef, potatoes, and cornbread.

As Torrin scraped together his last bite and popped it into his mouth, the bushes across from him rustled. Four small creatures emerged from the forest, blinking in the firelight.

The children stared at the unusual animals. They were about the size of badgers, but looked more like owls, with wide eyes like full moons and ears that stuck straight out to the sides with pointed ends. They were various shades of copper, gold, and silver, with shaggy fur that glimmered in the light.

Celeste gasped and huddled closer to Aunt Maggie.

Adelide tucked her feet a little further beneath her skirts, but otherwise kept her calm demeanor.

The largest one of these creatures waddled up to Aunt Maggie at her place at the fire.

"Why hello, Glimwhin," said Aunt Maggie. She broke off a piece of the cornbread she was eating and held it out to him.

Glimwhin reached out a little monkey-like hand and took the bread. He made a low trilling sound deep in his throat.

The other creatures crowded beside Aunt Maggie. She handed out food to all of them.

Lester swooped down and perched on Torrin's shoulder. "That is the tribe of Vooms," he murmured in Torrin's ear, tickling him dreadfully as he spoke. "We met them last time we were here. Fortunately, they speak Universal Beast, which I have taught to your Aunt Maggie."

"Huh," said Torrin, wishing Lester would teach him Universal Beast.

Glimwhin spoke to Aunt Maggie in what sounded like growls and chirps.

Aunt Maggie nodded and rubbed her chin, then responded with similar noises.

After a few more of these exchanges, Glimwhin gave a low bow and disappeared back into the forest, the other Vooms following him.

Aunt Maggie leaned against a tree and pursed her lips.

"Is everything all right, Aunt Maggie?" asked Jude.

"I hope so," she said, giving a quick smile. "Glimwhin said the Purrflyer king and queen are terribly sad. His Universal Beast is a bit hard for me to understand, so he couldn't tell me why, but he hopes we can help. The situation has cast a dark shadow over the entire kingdom."

"We helped the Eeps and Opes," said Celeste. "We stopped an entire war."

"And kept a flood from destroying two villages," put in Torrin.

"Did that really happen?" asked Adelide.

"It certainly did." Aunt Maggie beamed, her cheeks turning pink.

Adelide opened her mouth as though she wanted to say more, but instead she picked at a piece of bark on the tree trunk in front of her.

"I think we should be going to bed," Aunt Maggie announced. "You all know where your bedtime supplies are. Except for Adelide. Celeste, will you please show her the ropes?"

After the long trip and excitement from all the new discoveries, the children were thankful to pile into their snug little tents.

As the boys lay on their soft, warm beds made of Hewhover fronds, Jude said, "Adelide did better than I thought she would today."

"Yeah," Torrin replied. "But she's still really annoying. I'd enjoy the trip a lot more if she weren't with us."

"It would be nice if she wouldn't make so many personal remarks," Jude admitted. "But maybe it's like Aunt Maggie said. She's not used to being with other children. Maybe she'll change her attitude before the end of the trip."

"That would be nice, but I doubt it," said Torrin. He turned and closed his eyes, trying to imagine what the castle of the King of the Purrflyers would be like.

4

The Palace of the Purrflyers

Breakfast was finished and camp supplies put away, but Aunt Maggie made no move to load everyone back into the Windlesoar. She stood on the edge of the clearing, gazing at the distant mountains. Strands of long hair that had fallen from her bun drifted about her face in the restless breeze.

Torrin patted her on the shoulder. "What would you like us to do now, Aunt Maggie? Everything's ready to go."

Aunt Maggie spun to face him. "Why, didn't I tell you? We've already arrived. The Purrflyer castle is high on that mountain. I can't fly to the top, there's not a space big enough for the Windlesoar to land."

"Then I guess we should prepare for a hike?" asked Torrin.

"Not quite yet." Aunt Maggie lifted a hand to shade her eyes and searched the side of the mountain. "We have to wait. Lester's flying now to let the Purrflyers know that we've arrived. It's strange, I expected a scout to find us by this time."

"Won't Lester be in danger?" asked Torrin.

Aunt Maggie chuckled. "Absolutely not. The Purrflyers are no larger than ordinary house cats. None of them are strong enough to fight Lester. Besides, they know Lester's with me. He delivers messages back and forth from time to time."

Jude sat at the smoldering remains of the campfire, whittling on a little stick. Celeste knelt in the circle of singing flowers she'd woken again, humming along. Cousin Adelide perched on a rock a little way from the others, her hands folded primly in her lap, as usual.

A dark shape appeared in the sky. At first Torrin thought it was Lester, but then he realized the flight pattern was all wrong. This creature soared where Lester would have flapped, and his wings gleamed in the morning sun. As the flying beast approached the campsite, Torrin discovered it was, indeed, a flying cat.

The creature touched down lightly, wings folding on his back like those of a bird. He was a sleek, handsome fellow with inky black fur and silver wings.

Aunt Maggie held out her hand. "I see the king has received our message."

The cat dipped his head in a little bow. "Yes, Duchess Margarite. I am Harold."

Jude squinted at him. "Are you also a royal herald?"

"Certainly." The corners of Harold's mouth quirked up into a smile. "I'm from a long line of heralds, so the name saves time. I've been sent, Duchess, to fetch you and your party."

He regarded the four children. "Are they all with you?"

"Yes, Harold, this is my crew," said Aunt Maggie.

"Fine, fine." The cat waved his paw. "Please follow me. I will walk beside you to lead the way, you won't be able to keep up with me if I fly."

As everyone followed the glistening black cat, Lester dove from a tree and hung upside down from his usual travelling place on Aunt Maggie's back. Torrin caught him mumbling something about how cats shouldn't be allowed to have wings, too quiet for anyone else to hear.

The forest became dense and dark, with the sun barely peeping through the thick fronds of the Hewhover trees. Old leaves and crumbled bark covered the ground, and squishy marsh puddles dotted trail. The children were forced to step carefully or else risk soggy shoes, and everyone knows how miserable wet socks feel.

Strange animal calls floated through the trees, and a few times bright orange frog-like creatures leapt from the bushes and hopped across the road, too fast to study.

After a short walk, the forest thinned again, and the mountain rose before them, just a few hundred yards ahead. Torrin tipped his head back, but still couldn't see the castle at the top. Beside the mountain was a very wide column made of bricks.

"What's this thing for?" Jude rapped it with a fist.

"You shall see," said Aunt Maggie.

Harold bowed once more. "I shall return in a few moments."

The children sat on a cluster of rocks huddled together. All except for Adelide, who stood to the side, staring off into the distance.

"Will we have to climb the mountain?" Celeste asked, craning her neck to check out the side of the sheer cliff. She bit her lip.

"Goodness, no, child." Aunt Maggie patted her shoulder. "The mountain is far too steep for that. Just be patient."

A strange, squeaking noise started above them, faint and far away. It grew louder. Torrin cupped a hand behind his ear. What was that? Almost like an old wagon wheel, or the hinge of a rusted gate . . .

Jude pointed upward, and everyone's gaze followed his finger.

A large, rectangular thing was falling from the sky. Well, not falling, exactly. *Was it being lowered?* Yes, because as it came down Torrin could make out ropes fastened to the four corners, and another rope in the middle suspended it in the air . . . attached to what? *Too far to tell.*

The rectangular thing landed on the ground, dust flying from all sides.

"Oh!" Cousin Adelide shook the dirt from her skirts.

"All right children, follow me." Aunt Maggie climbed on to the platform and sat down, tucking her skirts and scarves beneath her.

"Do you think it's safe?" Celeste whispered to Torrin as they followed suit.

"Of course it's safe," Adelide answered for him, in a loud, indignant voice. "Duchess Margarite would never put us in danger!"

Torrin's face warmed. "She wasn't asking you!" he shouted, a bit louder than he intended.

"Children, please sit down!" Aunt Maggie snapped. "Harold is waiting for my signal."

Torrin obeyed and folded his arms, glowering at Adelide, who stuck her nose in the air and turned the other way.

That's it. I'm never going anywhere with her again.

Aunt Maggie tapped Lester. "Hey, I need you to go tell Harold we're all settled."

Lester's eyelids fluttered, and he smacked his lips. "All right, all right. I'm going." He flapped his wings and flew to the top of the mountain in lazy circles.

A few moments later the platform lurched. Soon it left the ground all together, swaying slightly.

"We're lucky there's not much of a breeze," said Aunt Maggie. "The trip is much more adventurous when you're hanging on for dear life." She folded her hands in her lap. "This is quite nice, actually."

The platform ascended higher and higher. The first few moments, the contraption was only a few feet off the ground, and Torrin could have jumped down without injury if he'd wanted to. But soon the trees grew smaller, and clouds crowded beneath them.

Now Torrin could tell the main rope was attached to some sort of long pole, running from the top of the giant column to somewhere on the peak of the mountain. An unseen force twisted the pole, which in turn shortened the rope. As the rope ran along the pole, the platform also travelled closer and closer to the mountain top.

They passed a rock shelf that had blocked the view. A giant crank came into view, with Purrflyers crowded about it, working together to turn the rope. Above the shelf rose a brilliant white castle, studded with beautiful stones in a rainbow of colors. The towers of the castle were partially hidden by mounds of fluffy clouds.

"It's so beautiful." Celeste clasped her hands.

"It is very nice," said Adelide.

When the platform was level with the rock ledge, there was still a gap of several feet. A dozen cats flew to the side of the platform. There were felines of all colors. Orange tabby cats, calicos, gray and white striped, and one Siamese cat with lovely wings the color of taffy.

These cats grasped the side of the platform with their paws and, hovering in the air, pushed it to the shelf, where another team shifted it to the solid rock.

Torrin stepped out with the others, his legs a bit shaky. As thrilling as the trip had been, it was nice to be on solid ground again.

Harold approached them in mincing steps. "I hope your journey was pleasant."

"Very," said Aunt Maggie.

Harold dipped his head. "I will be taking leave of you now. Persephone will be your guide in the palace."

A small, marmalade cat with a round, fluffy face darted out of the crowd of Purrflyers. "Welcome, royals," she said in a high voice. "You have been anxiously awaited. Please come with me and all shall be explained in the utmost of haste."

"Hello, Persephone, nice to see you again," said Aunt Maggie. "And these children are—"

Persephone held out a striped paw. "Please forgive my rudeness, but there isn't time." She turned and trotted up a little twisted path. "Please come as quickly as you can. We have a light luncheon for you, where all shall be explained."

"All right." Aunt Maggie motioned to the children, and they followed the pretty little cat along the narrow route.

On and on they went. Only a few scraggly trees and bushes grew on the rocky trail, but these were quite amazing on their own. One type of bush had star-shaped golden leaves that glowed, and another sported purple flowers, shaped like plump balloons, swaying in the breeze. When Torrin poked at one, it popped off its twig and floated away.

After a quick hike they approached the castle walls. Several cats awaited them at the gates.

"Give them a few moments," said Persephone. "The gates haven't been used for quite some time, as we cats use the upper windows. We have freshly oiled them this morning and it shouldn't take too long." She nodded to the sturdy cats on either side of the gate, and the feathered felines pushed and pulled at cranks attached to ropes. After a bit of straining and groaning on the part of the cats, the gates began to crack open.

Jude watched with one eyebrow raised. "It's all very scientific, isn't it?"

"Yes." Aunt Maggie nodded. "I've learned a thing or two from these flying cats. Their studies in physics is one of the reasons I came to visit them in the first place, long ago."

"That's enough!" Persephone called out in her high, velvety voice. "The humans can fit through now." She turned to the group. "Please forgive our hasty arrangements. The kingdom is in a state of despair and only the leanest accommodations have been cobbled together. Please don't take this as a measurement of our gratitude for your arrival."

"Of course not," said Aunt Maggie as they followed Persephone into the castle.

The castle walls vaulted several stories above their heads, lit by torches on the sides and sunlight spilling in from windows every few feet. There were no inside doors, only porthole-like openings in the sides at various levels where cats moved in and out.

Of course, why would they have doors? Too difficult to open and close.

All along the walls were wide shelves of various lengths and widths, and on these shelves, cats napped, talked, or batted at shiny things hanging from strings.

Colored stones had been embedded in cement to make pictures of butterflies and flowers on the castle floor.

A sleek ginger kitty strolled by, pushing a broom in front of him with his nose. Clumps of cat hair were piled in front.

Persephone turned to the group. "My apologies. They were supposed to have everything cleaned before you arrived."

"Quite all right," Aunt Maggie murmured.

Persephone headed to a golden double door with an arched top. "Here we are. This way, please."

A long table filled this room, with half-a-dozen human sized chairs gathered on one end. The table was set for eight. Cats bustled to and fro with covered dishes and large, foaming pitchers of milk.

"Please, sit." Persephone waved a paw to the chairs. Aunt Maggie sat at the foot of the table and the children found chairs near her.

Persephone jumped up next to Torrin, taking care not to hit him in the face with her folded wings. "Pardon me for sitting on the table, but cats can't eat the same way you humans do," she said.

"Quite all right," said Torrin. "It's your kingdom."

Smoke curled from the dishes in the center of the table, and Torrin's stomach rumbled. Breakfast seemed like a lifetime ago.

Cats fluttered around the table, serving food from small dishes that hung by handles from their jaws.

Torrin studied the food on his plate. A whole roasted fish, complete with the head. A pile of mashed potatoes. And a glass of milk.

Fish wouldn't normally be Torrin's first choice for supper, but he was far too hungry to complain. Celeste, Jude and Adelide dug into their food as well. Torrin heard Adelide actually smack her lips once, which was ridiculously satisfying.

As they all continued to eat, a distant fanfare sounded. Two cats appeared in one of the curious portholes, about fifteen feet up in the wall. They flew down to the head of the table.

One was gold and white, with gleaming white wings, and the other was much larger and black with white splotches, with black wings. They both wore thin, golden circlets over their heads, balanced behind their ears.

Persephone bowed from her place on the table. "May I introduce their royal highnesses, King Winsome and Queen Maribelle."

The children and Aunt Maggie rose. The boys bowed and the girls curtseyed.

The King and Queen of the Purrflyers gave bows of their own.

"We are honored you have come," said the king, in a voice that was quite booming for a cat.

"Please eat." The queen nodded to their half-empty plates. "My husband and I are too sad to join you."

Aunt Maggie set down her fork. "We are sorry to hear that. Can you please explain what happened?"

The Queen covered her face with a paw. "I cannot speak of it."

"It is the most horrible thing that could happen to a king and queen," said King Winsome. "Our dear children, Prince David and Princess Dania, have disappeared."

"Oh no." Aunt Maggie walked around the table and patted the Queen's tiny white paw. "Whatever happened to them?"

"We don't know." Queen Maribelle wailed. "They disappeared without a trace five days ago. We've searched everywhere. They only just started flying, you know. Their quill feathers grew in last month."

"They were forbidden to fly past the mountains." The king straightened and stretched out his wings. "All the kittens are, until they turn a year old. The kittens were only six months. Twins."

"Yes." Aunt Maggie nodded. "My last visit was right after they were born. They didn't even have their eyes open. My, they were adorable, the little mewing darlings." She wiped a tear from the corner of her eye. "And to think they are missing!"

Torrin glanced at Jude. It was quite strange to think of kittens flying away at only six months old, but of course kittens and humans grew at different rates. *It must be the same for flying cats as well.*

"So you have no idea where they went?" asked Jude.

"We can't imagine. Our strongest scouts have been out searching, night and day." The King curled his tail around his feet. "I'd be gone myself, but I injured my wing the first day the children disappeared. The royal doctor said if I tried to fly before it heals, I'll fall right out of the sky."

"Which wouldn't do anyone any good," the Queen put in.

"The kittens didn't leave a note or anything?" asked Celeste.

The Queen frowned. "Not that we've found. We did wonder . . ."

The King held up his paw. "Now, Darling, you know they would never take such a risk."

"But my birthday is in a few days," said the Queen. "And I said that foolish, foolish thing."

"What foolish thing?" asked Adelide, who had been silent up until now.

"Only that . . . I've always loved the salt sculptures made by the Gnomes of Glinder." The Queen covered her face with a paw. "And Dania . . . she's such a thoughtful little kitten, said she wanted to fetch me one."

"But our children could never journey there," said the King. "The mountain winds are too strong. They would have been blown off course."

"Perhaps they walked some of the way?" asked Aunt Maggie. "I mean, in the places with the strongest winds."

The King's eyes widened into two emerald globes. "We hadn't thought of that." He glanced at the Queen. "It would be possible. A journey of walking and flying combined. They could have reached the gnomes in less than a day."

"In that case, there's no time to waste." Aunt Maggie picked her napkin from her lap and placed it on the plate before her. "We shall fly over the mountain. I've equipped the Windlesoar to handle strong winds, it shouldn't be a problem."

The Queen sighed. "Why didn't we think of them walking before?"

Aunt Maggie chuckled. "I've learned not to underestimate children. It only wastes time. You're new parents. You can't be expected to think of everything."

The King frowned. "But if they went to the gnomes, why haven't they returned? The gnomes work fast, even a custom sculpture wouldn't have taken more than a day. The kittens should have been home two days ago, at the very latest."

The Queen began to cry again. "Oh, they've probably been eaten by a hawk. Or a dragon! My poor babies."

A tear glistened on Celeste's cheek, and Torrin rather felt like crying himself. He tried to imagine how his parents would feel if their three children disappeared without a trace. *They must trust Aunt Maggie so much to let us go on adventures with her.*

"Another reason we must leave in haste." Aunt Maggie said. "Children, let's prepare the Windlesoar without delay. We shall visit the Gnomes of Glinder. With any luck, the prince and princess will be waiting for us there."

5

Meeting the Gnomes

By the time the Windlesoar had once again taken flight, Torrin was too tired to keep his eyes open, much less bicker with Adelide. He dozed off, only to be jerked awake by the basket, which dipped and plunged through the air like a bucking steed (which is a princely word for horse).

Adelide clutched the sides of her seat until her knuckles turned white. She bit her lip, as though trying to hold back a scream.

Torrin felt a teensy bit sorry for her. "Don't worry," he finally said. "Aunt Maggie has been flying the

Windlesoar for years. She can handle it. And I'm sure we'll be landing in a few minutes."

Adelide stared at him. "Those children should have known better than to wander off like they did. If something bad happened to them, they got what they deserved. We shouldn't be going after them. Wild goose chases are improper for young royals."

"How can you say that?" A lump formed in Torrin's throat. "How would you feel if something happened to us and the Royal Army refused to search for us?"

"That's completely different." Adelide lifted her chin. "The Royal Army's job is to search for royals in trouble."

"What about being ambassadors of peace and goodwill and learning about the surrounding kingdoms?" Torrin folded his arms.

"My papa wouldn't approve of me flying into danger in this way. I was assured this trip would be completely safe. I've been in rumbly wagons but never in something that felt like it might fall right out of the sky. I'm beginning to wonder if the Duchess is quite right in her head."

Torrin rested his chin in his hands and did not reply. The basket continued to jolt and soar in an alarming fashion. He really hoped he was right and Aunt Maggie knew what she was doing.

Thankfully, right then came the familiar dip of the Windlesoar's descent which ended when the basket landed on the ground with a gentle thump.

Torrin let out a long breath. "We made it."

"Yes." Adelide coughed. "I hope that's the craziest thing that happens. Though I'm beginning to think the Duchess is not safe."

"That's it." Torrin spoke through clenched teeth. "No one asked you to come on this trip. In fact we warned you not to. Aunt Maggie hasn't let us down yet. If you get hurt, or I don't know, tear your dress, then you can complain. But right now I don't want to hear any more about it."

"I was merely speaking facts," said Adelide. "It's unbecoming for royals to complain."

"I give up." Torrin stretched his arms and lifted the lid off the basket.

Gone were the lovely trees and the singing flowers. The land surrounding the Windlesoar was desolate and bare. Stretching before them was another mountain, but this one was solid rock, with no bushes or trees to adorn the ledges. A rainbow of colors shone from the sides, glittering in spots where the sun touched them.

"Let's go." Aunt Maggie's face was drawn, and her eyelids sagged as though she were very, very tired. "I've never been here before, so I'm not sure where the entrance is. I know the gnomes are friendly; hopefully they will welcome us and assist in finding the kittens."

"Maybe the kittens are inside waiting for us," Celeste said brightly.

"Let's hope so," said Aunt Maggie. But her shoulders slumped as they walked towards the side of the mountain.

"I wonder if Aunt Maggie thinks the kittens are alive," Jude whispered to Torrin.

"I don't know. They must have been awfully small when she saw them. Remember when the stable cat had kittens last year? I could cup one in my hand," said Torrin.

As he said this, a loud grating noise came from the mountain. A slab of rock, much higher than Aunt Maggie's head, cracked apart and slid away from the surface of the hill.

"Is it an earthquake?" yelled Celeste.

"I don't think so," Aunt Maggie shouted back. "Look!" She pointed to the crack, which yawned open further and further.

Three people emerged from the opening. They were squat, stout and wrapped in robes of crystal blue with silver sparkles. Their heads were topped with curious, cone-shaped hats, with long golden tassels drooping from the pointed ends. Each one had a long, thin beard and wisps of hair falling down their backs.

The tallest one, who came just to Aunt Maggie's waist, bowed deeply. "Greetings," he said in a gravelly voice. "We are the Glimmer gnomes. I'm Gloom, this is Groom," he pointed to the medium-sized gnome. "And he's Gnoom." The shortest gnome waved.

Gloom cleared his throat and continued. "We assume you have come to order a carving. We promise you will find no finer salt sculptures in the entire realm of Krispinland."

Aunt Maggie returned the bow. "Hello, I am Duchess Margarite, and this is Princess Celeste, Princess Adelide, Prince Jude and Prince Torrin. I'm sure your carvings are second to none. However, we've come under much more grave circumstances. We're searching for the royal Purrflyer children, Prince David and Princess Dania. Did they come here?"

Groom scratched his beard. "You mean the kitties? Yes."

"We're actually wondering where they went off to," Gnoom piped up. "We finished their carving two days ago, and they paid in advance, but they never returned to fetch it."

"And you have no idea where they would have gone?" asked Aunt Maggie.

Gloom shrugged. "We provided them with a room to stay, and all the cream and fish they wanted. We get our provisions from a village on the other side of the mountain. But after the second day, they didn't come to dinner anymore."

"We thought perhaps they didn't like the sculpture and were too embarrassed to say anything." Groom's eyebrows narrowed. "No one has ever had such a problem with our work, but there's always a first time."

"You mean, you didn't send anyone to search for them?" Aunt Maggie's jaw was clenched, and there was an angry edge to her tone Torrin had never heard before.

Gloom glanced at his fellow gnomes. "Well, your–duchessness, as you can see, none of us possess wings. We figured we wouldn't be able to find them anyhow. And we have precious little time."

"Precious little!" Groom echoed, with an affirming nod. "People come from all the kingdoms of the world for Glimmer gnome carvings."

Aunt Maggie sighed and turned to the children, her hands raised. "I'm at a loss. I really don't know how we'll find them. We can send Lester out to sweep these hills, but his eyesight is poor and his sense of smell can only go so far."

Torrin tapped Aunt Maggie's shoulder. "Can we at least see where the prince and princess were staying? Maybe we'll find some sort of clue."

Aunt Maggie slowly nodded. "You're right, Torrin. We should at least try."

"You're welcome to come and and look." Gloom stepped aside. "While you're here you can see some of our amazing creations."

Groom added, "You should feel ever so fortunate. Kings and queens from everywhere in the world have taken treacherous journeys and crossed countless mountains to see the wonders of this cavern."

The children stepped into the cave. They followed the three gnomes and Aunt Maggie through a long, narrow passageway.

Torrin's mouth fell open.

The cavern's ceiling stretched even higher than the Purrflyer's castle. The walls were lit by blazing torches, immersed in vases of oil. Everywhere the light touched were glittering, sparkling carvings. Sculptures of birds, and horses, elves and wizards, and everything else you could possibly imagine. Clustered around these carvings were dozens more of the gnomes, beating away with hammers and chiseling with chisels. All wore the same robes and tasseled hats as the three that had welcomed the children.

The air was filled with the sounds of steel striking salt and the hums of the Glimmer Gnomes, which were probably supposed to be songs but sounded more like the deep thrumming of a hive of giant bees.

Groom, Gloom and Gnoom led them past a roped-off section, where many glistening salt carvings had been placed.

"These are the finished products, awaiting the proud owners' reception," said Groom, gesturing grandly with a sweep of his arm. "Of course, the royal kittens could never travel with something like this." He pointed to a life-sized elephant. "And they have no magic. So their carving was quite small."

Gnoom selected a bright white figurine about the size of Torrin's thumb. Everyone leaned in closer to get a better view.

The salt had been shaped into two perfect kittens, their wings unfurled to create a heart. Every feather was ornately formed, Torrin could even make out minute whiskers on each kitten's face.

THE THREE ROYAL CHILDREN AND THE BATTY AUNT

"Oh, it's beautiful," breathed Celeste.

"The sculptors in MY kingdom . . ." Adelide began, but Aunt Maggie put a finger to her lips and made a warning noise in her throat.

Adelide puffed out her cheeks but clamped her mouth shut.

"Yes, they're very nice," said Torrin.

A satisfied smile spread across Gloom's face. "Of course they are. Now, Gnoom will show you to the kitten's room."

Gnoom led them on through the massive cavern, and then darted to the right, down another long, darker passageway. Little doors were built in the rock, to the right and left.

"These are rooms for visitors. Sometimes we have several staying with us, but this is our quiet season," Gnoom explained. He waved a torch as they passed the doors. "Let's see. Room 17, 18 . . . Ah, here we are. Room 19."

He opened the door. As the group walked in, he lit a lamp on a shelf with his torch.

Torrin studied the space. Two small beds, with dark blue blankets and fluffy pillows. Shelves with books, and a small desk with a chair completed the furniture.

Aunt Maggie examined a pillow. "Looks cozy."

"We want our guests to be comfortable," said Gnoom.

"What's this?" Celeste showed them a piece of cloth. "I found it beside the bed."

Torrin examined the small, soft square of faded pink material. The fuzz had been mostly worn off, as though the owner had rubbed their cheeks on it every night.

"I know what this is," he said. "It's a blankie."

"Oh. You're right," said Celeste. "Of course."

Torrin knew Celeste would understand, because all three of the royal children had slept with their own special bedtime blankies for many years. Of course, they were all too old for such things now, but every now and then he would find a box in the top of his wardrobe, pull out his old, tattered blanket, and rub it on his cheek.

He showed the fabric to Aunt Maggie. "The kittens never left the cavern," he said. "They wouldn't have gone without their blankie. It's too precious to leave behind."

Gnoom bowed his head. "If you are correct, then I know where they might have gone. But we tell our guests specifically to never enter the cavern to his lair. It's much too dangerous."

"What cavern? Who's lair?" asked Jude.

Gnoom's forehead creased beneath his fancy tassel hat. "The lair of the cave troll."

6

A Dangerous Journey

"How dangerous is this cave troll?" asked Aunt Maggie. The group had left the kittens' room and were gathered in the dim passageway again.

"Well, he's ginormous." Gnoom rubbed the end of his knobby nose. "Taller than the tallest human I've met. He goes to the surrounding villages and steals things all the time. The humans have discussed putting together a mob to arrest him and put him in jail, but let's face it, they aren't the bravest bunch. He doesn't bother us, because he can't fit through the passageway under the mountain and our front entrance is well guarded. We have skills in locksmithing as well as salt carving." Gnoom blinked rapidly. "Why, oh why would those kittens go down that passage?"

"Curiosity killed the cat," Lester said sleepily from his perch.

Gnoom frowned. "I've never heard of the troll actually hurting anyone. He usually gives a roar, and everyone runs away. If the kittens wandered into his cave, he probably wouldn't harm them. But he might have kitten-napped them."

"That's it." Aunt Maggie squared her shoulders. "Gnoom, take me to the passageway. Children, you must stay here with the gnomes until I return."

Jude lifted his chin. "If you go, we go, Aunt Maggie."

"Hey, I faced a Growlie," said Torrin. "I'm not afraid of some cave troll."

"I can run really fast," said Celeste. "Gnoom said the Troll can't fit in the passageway, so we can always escape if we have to."

Everyone looked at Adelide.

"I–" she sighed. "It's unbecoming to young royals to be cowards."

"So be it." Aunt Maggie said. "We began this adventure together, and we will continue as a team."

Gnoom's eyes flickered past all their faces. "If you are absolutely sure, I'll guide you to the entrance. We're required to show the tunnel to every guest anyway, so people won't explore it by mistake. Pay close attention, if you don't know the trick it's easy to get lost."

"What's the trick?" asked Torrin.

"If you want to get back to the main carving cavern, follow the green lights." Gnoom pointed to the flickering torches, and Torrin realized, for the first time, they were indeed slightly tinged with green. "The purple lights lead to the lair of the troll."

He shuffled down the tunnel, and they followed.

The sound of dripping water surrounded them, and many droplets landed on Torrin's head. One particularly large drop splattered on the end of his nose.

The passageway opened into another large room, though not so large as the carving cavern. Torch light played on the surface of a cavern pool.

"Why, it's green," said Celeste.

"Minerals in the rocks." Jude knelt and stuck his finger in the water. "At least, I think that's what it is."

"Good job, Jude," said Aunt Maggie. "Very scientific."

Gnoom went to a rock beside the pool where a large wooden chest was waiting. He flipped back the lid, almost knocking off his tapered hat in the process. "The path to the troll's lair is long. You'll need some basic supplies." He handed everyone a torch and a canteen. "The water throughout the cavern is safe to drink. You can fill your canteens here, and you'll find several more pools along the way. Do you need food?"

"No, thank you. We have dried fruit, biscuits and meat in our packs." Aunt Maggie patted the satchel that hung beside Lester.

"In that case I shall bid you farewell." Gnoom folded his fingers together. "Take care, and do not underestimate the cave troll. He has a nasty temper, and not much of a conscience."

"Hopefully we won't see him at all," said Aunt Maggie. "Thank you for your help, Gnoom."

A silvery tear ran down Gnoom's wrinkled cheek. "I hope you can find the kittens," he said. "I would have gone after them myself if I'd suspected they went down that tunnel. But you must believe, we were sure they flew away. They are children after all. Us gnomes are hundreds of years old. We don't have any children and we don't remember being children. So they are a mystery to us."

Aunt Maggie patted his gnarled hand. "I understand. I'm sure we'll find them if they are to be found."

Gnome slunk back down the passageway, following the green lights.

"I still think the gnomes were cowards not to search for the kittens." Adelide grabbed a canteen from the pile and dipped it into the pond.

Torrin's eye twitched. "First you think the kittens were wrong to run away, and now you think the Gnomes were wrong to not go after them. Do you ever think people make good choices?"

"Yes. I think we are right to at least try to find them. We've been asked, by a king, for help and we should do our royal duty."

Torrin heard an exasperated sigh behind him. He whirled around, expecting it to be Jude or Celeste, but it was Aunt Maggie. He caught her mid eye-roll. She blinked quickly and gave a sheepish smile.

It happened. Cousin Adelide is finally getting to her. She should never have asked her to come.

"Can we please not fight anymore?" Celeste begged. "A long journey lies ahead of us, and I'm trying not to feel scared. Can we please at least try to be nice to each other?"

Torrin gave a gusty sigh and filled his canteen.

Jude led the way through the passage. Only a few of the torches at the beginning were lit, so soon they had to rely on the ones they held for their sole light. The flames flickered and danced on the walls, making strange unworldly shadows.

A bat much smaller then Lester, swooped down above their heads. Lester squeaked something. The bat squeaked in return and flew away.

"Did he know anything about the kittens?" asked Aunt Maggie.

"Yes," Lester replied. "Said they flew through here three days ago. Scared him and his family near to death. The kittens were far too small to catch them, but they were worried the bigger ones would be coming as well. His entire family is in hiding. They sent him out as a scout. He wouldn't have shown himself, but he smelled me and wondered why I was with a bunch of humans."

"You said all that in those few squeaks?" asked Jude.

"Animal languages are very different." Lester folded his wings a little tighter about himself. "We can say more in a few sounds than humans can say in an hour's worth of conversation. Saves a great deal of time"

"The good news is, the kittens did come this way," said Aunt Maggie. "We're on the right track."

The group walked on for what seemed to Torrin like hours, though it was hard to tell since they were in a dark place with no sun or sky to show the passage of daylight.

Jude had his pocket watch with him, but finally got annoyed with everyone asking him what time it was. He refused to check it after a while.

Torrin's stomach rumbled.

"These smooth stones look comfortable." Aunt Maggie stopped and gestured to the ground. "And not too damp. Why don't we sit and eat?"

Torrin sank down on a stone gratefully. His legs ached. He hoped they wouldn't have to go much farther. *But what will happen if the cave troll is home?*

"Do you think the cave troll is bigger than a growlie?" he whispered to Jude, who was chewing on a dried fig.

"Huh." Jude tilted his head. "I hope not. At least I'm sure his teeth can't be as long and sharp."

"Aunt Maggie, what is a troll?" asked Celeste.

"They're sort of like gnomes, since they prefer to be underground, but bald with no beards. Taller than people. The ones I've met haven't been particularly mean." Aunt Maggie took a sip from her canteen. "It's not nice to say, but they aren't very bright."

"You mean they're stupid?" asked Adelide.

"Calling people stupid is not becoming for young royals," said Torrin, with a great sense of satisfaction.

"Torrin's right." Aunt Maggie buttered a roll. "I don't think that's the correct word, at any rate. Trolls are focused on one thing, and one certain thing only. Some of them are always hungry, so their entire lives are spent finding and eating food."

Celeste's face went white. "Not people, right?"

"Of course not," said Aunt Maggie.

"Trolls eat people food, not people for food," said Lester.

Jude stood, brushed crumbs off his lap and ambled to the edge of the larger room they were in. "The tunnel gets narrower this way," he said, his voice echoing off the walls. "Hey, do you all hear that?"

"What?" Celeste went and cupped a hand behind her ear. "I don't hear anything."

Torrin followed Celeste, with Adelide next. They all leaned in, listening.

"Be careful!" Aunt Maggie called after them.

This cavern was the narrowest of all. Torren could touch both sides at once when he stretched out his fingers as far as they could go.

Jude held up his hand. "You guys can't hear that? It sounds like . . ."

"Mewing." Adelide nodded. "Yes, I see what you mean."

They pressed in further. The mews grew louder but now they formed into words. "Help! Please help!"

"Aunt Maggie, I think we hear the kittens!" shouted Celeste.

Jude grabbed her shoulder. "Be careful! Remember, we're in a cave!"

"What do you mean?" asked Celeste.

Jude opened his mouth but before he could speak, something rumbled above his head. Small bits of rock fell from the ceiling, a few at first and then more and more. The children screamed and covered their heads with their arms.

"This way." Celeste pulled on Torrin's sleeve. He found Adelide's hand in the dark and they all pushed through the narrow cavern together, away from Aunt Maggie and towards the mewing.

Bigger chunks of rock bounced from the ceiling. They wove their way through the debris, not daring to stop and check behind them.

"Ouch!" exclaimed Celeste. She held a hand to her cheek. A small trickle of blood flowed beneath her fingers.

"We have to keep going," Torrin urged her.

After several frightening minutes of running, dodging and running some more, the rocks stopped falling. Everything was deathly quiet.

Somehow, Jude had managed to keep his torch lit. He swung around, the light playing across everyone's dusty faces.

"Are you all okay?" he asked. Tears glinted in the corners of his eyes.

"I–I think so." Celeste pulled her hand away from her face. "Is it bad?"

Torrin examined her cheek. "It's a small cut. We'll clean it and you'll be fine."

Celeste took a shaky breath. "Okay."

Adelide shook out her dress, creating a larger dust cloud in the one that remained. "I'm as fine as can be expected. But what do we do now?"

The children surveyed the way they had come. What had been a narrow passage was now a solid wall of crumbled rock.

7

Captured Kittens

Torrin sank down to the floor, along with Celeste. A lump filled his throat, and for the first time in a very long time, tears threatened to spill down his cheeks. The cavern seemed so closed, so forever. And the space between the children and Aunt Maggie, the gnomes, and safety seemed as though it might as well be a million miles.

Tears streamed down Celeste's face, mixing with streaks of dust and blood. "I want Mama," she wailed. "Jude, help me get to Mama."

"Shush!" Jude said sharply.

Celeste's eyes widened, and she shut her mouth like a trap. Jude never talked like that unless it was important.

Jude held the torch high with one hand and put a finger to his lips. "I heard the mewing again."

Everyone held their breath and sat perfectly still.

"Mewwww! Mewwww! Help us! Help us!" The voices were high and faint, but definitely there, and coming from the end of the passage.

"Come on!" Jude darted down the tunnel.

"Wait, what if there's another cave in?" asked Celeste.

"And what if Aunt Maggie and Lester are . . . hurt?" Torrin couldn't bring himself to suggest anything worse.

Jude peered back at them. "We aren't going to get anywhere trying to dig through that rock. We'll have to try to find another way out of here."

Adelide nodded. "Quite right. Let's move on. It's unbecoming to young royals to cry and wail about things they can't change." She gave Celeste a hard stare.

Celeste stuck out her tongue, but she rose and followed everyone else.

"It's unbecoming to young royals . . . oh, never mind." Adelide sighed and trudged after Jude.

The passage twisted sharply to the left, then right, then left again. As the group rounded the fourth corner, Torrin blinked and rubbed his eyes. *Could it be?*

"Light!" Celeste stumbled forward. "We must have found the troll's house!"

Jude grabbed her elbow and jerked her back. "Hush!" he hissed again. "If it's the troll's lair, *then the troll might be in there.*"

"What?" Celeste whispered loudly. A fresh tear rolled down her cheek and dripped off the edge of her nose.

"Calm down," Torrin told her. "The troll can't fit in this passage, remember? We'll be okay."

Jude crept forward, watching the ground for loose stones, the torch held low over the cavern floor. None of the others had their own torch, so everyone else made dreadful crunching and snapping noises, no matter how quiet they tried to be.

The light brightened and grew as they drew nearer, and the pitiful mews and cries for help became louder.

The children stepped into a room filled with torchlight. Piles of crates and wooden boxes partially blocked the opening.

Jude flattened himself against a crate and scooted beside it, peeking out. He motioned for everyone else to stay behind, then disappeared around the pile.

Torrin's heart hammered against his ribs. *What if Jude is captured by the troll? What if I never see him again?*

"Come on, guys," Jude said in a normal voice. "The troll isn't here, but guess who I found?"

The two girls went first. Torrin drew his wooden practice dagger from its sheath and followed behind.

The cavern was big enough to hold a reasonably-sized cottage, chimney and all. Furniture was piled by the walls, along with, books, statues, and even open chests of glittering–jewels? Torrin couldn't tell. The air was filled with a musty scent of old, forgotten things.

"Are you sure it's safe?" he called out.

"Come see for yourself," Jude called back.

Enormous shelves lined one wall, wide enough for a grown man to lay on if they hadn't been stuffed full of odds and ends. Wedged between these shelves was a wire enclosure. It reminded Torrin of the cages in the royal aviaries that held the king's collection of exotic birds from the four corners of the Earth. In the corner of this cage shivered two tiny kittens with wings folded on their backs.

One of the kittens was yellow and white, and one black and white, just like the king and queen. They pushed their furry faces to the bars and mewed. "Hello, hello! Help us! Rescue us!"

"We'll do our best," said Torrin. "But what about the troll?"

"He's away," said the black and white kitten, who had a high, sweet voice and long eyelashes, and was most certainly Princess Dania. "He skulks out every day to steal things from the villagers nearby. Sometimes he goes even farther if he can't find something he wants."

"What does he steal?" asked Princess Celeste.

"Look about you," said the other kitten, Prince David. "Everything here, from the largest statue to the tiniest jewel, has been stolen from somewhere nearby, as far as we can guess."

"Even us," put in Princess Dania. "Can you please help us?"

"Please, please!" Prince David pressed his furry face to the bars.

"We'll do our best." Prince Jude pointed to a padlock at the cage's door that was bigger than the kittens themselves. "Do you know where the key is?"

Princess Dania frowned. "Yes, but the troll keeps it on a rope around his neck. I don't know how you could get it from him."

"He's so big and mean." Prince David covered his eyes with his paws.

Torrin wondered if they really could save the kittens. *What if the troll tries to hurt us? What if we can't get the cage unlocked?*

Then an even more terrible thought rose in his mind. *What if the troll captures us and puts us in the cage too?*

He glanced at his siblings. They wore worried frowns as well. Only Adelide seemed calm and collected.

"Why don't we check here?" Adelide said. "This cavern is filled to the gills with stuff. There's bound to be something we can use to pry the bars apart or open the cage."

"Good idea," said Torrin, a bit grudgingly. A lantern was flickering from a nearby shelf. He took this and circled the room, studying the endless junk that filled every surface and corner.

The other children did likewise.

"What about this?" Celeste held up a broom.

Jude shook his head. "Too flimsy. It could get broken and then the troll might notice."

"What about that thing over there? Hanging from the wall?" Adelide pointed to a metal bar with a rough surface and a handle on one end.

"A file? What luck!" Jude breathed. He pulled it down and brought it to the bars. "This should do nicely!"

Princess Dania made a face. "The troll uses that on his nasty toenails."

"Well, we're going to use it to get you out of here." Jude began to rub it against the bars. Sparks flew, and a terrible screeching sound filled the room. Torrin covered his ears.

Jude examined the bars. "Hmmm. This file is big and sharp. It should easily cut through here. I wonder what's going on?"

"Let me try." Torrin took the file and grated it against the bars until his fingers hurt. But it was no use. The metal stayed strong and shiny as ever, without so much as a mark.

Adelide held a light by the cage. "See how these bars are blue and sparkle in the light? I think this might be a special metal made by the elves of Oom. I visited them once, with my papa. So far, no one has ever found anything that could break it."

Jude stepped back. "Oh dear."

A deep, booming voice echoed through the cavern, making everyone jump.

"Kittens! I'm back! I brought you a treat!"

Heavy footsteps approached, becoming louder and louder.

"Hurry, put everything away and hide!" cried Dania. "The troll will be here in a second!"

The children scrambled to place the items they'd been using exactly the way they'd been found. Then everyone piled into the cavern, scooting as far back as possible.

Torrin felt as though his heart would leap out of his throat. Celeste's fingers gripped his hand.

"Don't be scared," he whispered. He hoped she couldn't tell he was shivering. "Even if the troll saw us, he can't get to us in here. The gnomes said he was too big."

"Hello, my kittens," the troll's voice boomed again. "Look at the pretty collars I found for you today! Stole 'em from a rich lady."

Bars rattled, and Torrin figured the troll must be opening the kitten's cage.

"Here's one with emeralds for you, little David. And one with rubies for you, my dear Dania."

Torrin clapped a hand over his mouth. The troll didn't sound mean. His voice was kind. *Why would he bring gifts for the kittens if he was so frightful?*

"Mr. Troll, Sir," came Prince David's voice. "The collars are very pretty. But my sister and I don't want to wear collars. We're royal children, sir. Not pets."

The troll roared with laughter. "Ooh hoo, royal children, are you? Not anymore. You came into my cave. Now you belong to me. You have to be my friends because I say so."

"But–Mr. Troll." Princess Dania's voice quivered. "We want to go home. Our mama and papa miss us."

"That's not going to happen," said the troll. "See here. If I let you go, then I'll miss you. And we can't have that. Then I won't have any friends. What about me?"

As mean as the troll was being, Torrin felt a tiny wave of pity for him. *How would I feel if I lived in a deep cave and didn't have anyone to care about me? Of course, if the troll wasn't so mean and nasty, he probably would have more friends.* He glanced at Adelide, who was straining to listen. *Does Adelide have any friends?* He shrugged. *Probably not, with her attitude.*

"My little pets, your new collars are nice," the troll said. "Back into your cage you go!"

Despite the kittens' protests, the children heard the clanging of the door, followed by the snap of the padlock.

"Enjoy your gifts, my little friends." The troll yawned. "I'm going to take a nap before I go out to steal more things."

The children sat still for what seemed like a very, very long time. Drops of sweat dripped down Torrin's face, but he didn't dare to wipe them away.

Finally, a rumbling noise came from the direction of the troll's lair. A deep, thundering sound that shook the ground beneath the children's feet. The troll was snoring.

Jude put a finger to his lips and crept out into the cavern. Torrin was right at his heels, and the girls followed.

The troll sprawled out on the floor. The gnomes hadn't exaggerated. He was truly enormous, much bigger than even a growlie. His bare feet, ending in thick yellow toenails, almost blocked the children's tunnel.

Celeste squeezed her nose shut as they crept by.

The kittens' eyes widened as the children moved past the cage.

"Be careful," whispered Dania.

They passed the troll's knobby knees, his midsection and then his chest, which heaved with each shuddering snore. The troll's face was most frightful. His eyes were closed, and his mouth wide open, full of rotten teeth.

Hanging from his neck, just like the kittens had said, was a glittering key. But none of the children were tall enough to reach.

"One of us will have to climb and get it," Jude hissed. "But how can we do it without waking him?"

Torrin gestured to a ladder leaning against the wall. Celeste pressed her hand to her head, then pointed to a chair. Jude nodded.

The children worked together to move the chair to the troll as quietly as possible. Jude climbed the ladder, then Celeste climbed the chair and took Jude's hand. When she leaned over, she could almost reach the key–but not quite. She glared at the troll and climbed down from the chair.

Torrin did the same thing Celeste had done, grasping Jude's hand tightly. Jude leaned out as far as he could go, allowing Torrin to stretch out farther. As Torrin's fingers found the key, he felt the edge of the chair slip beneath him.

With a crash the chair landed on the floor. Torrin's fingers slipped from Jude's grasp, and he landed on the troll's chest with a thump.

Torrin froze. Every muscle in his body was like stone, and he felt like the heaviest person in all the world. He stared at the key, just out of his reach, then at the troll's closed eyes.

The fringe of lashes, thick as hairbrush bristles, fluttered, then stilled.

Jude still hung from the ladder, his face white as Prince David's feather's. "Get the key," he mouthed.

Inch by inch, Torrin moved his hand toward the key. He'd have to move his whole body to reach it, just a little further . . .

His foot slipped and his heel dug into one of the troll's ribs.

The troll chuckled in his sleep. "Don't tickle. Bless me, don't tickle," he muttered in his sleep.

A hand, with fingers as thick as a grown man's leg, swept towards Torrin. He ducked and lost his footing, tumbling to the floor.

Jude scurried down the ladder, as quick as a wink, and the four children ran back to the side passage as fast as their feet would take them.

"Who's here!" bellowed the troll, fully awake now.

The children huddled together in the darkness.

Torrin panted for breath, trying to regulate his breathing. He was certain the troll would hear them. *He can't get us. He's too big,* he reminded himself. But if they were discovered, they would lose any chance of escape, or rescuing the kittens. *We'd have to come out sometime.*

"What's going on?" the troll shouted, his voice booming through the cavern. "What's all this mess?"

"A big spider crawled on your chest while you were sleeping," came Princess Dania's voice. "It must have tickled. You thrashed about something awful."

"Oooh, I hate spiders," the troll grumbled. "Did you see where it went?" A loud crashing and banging followed, as though the troll were trashing the cavern. "I'll smash it to oblivion."

"I think it went outside," Prince David said.

"Well, fine," said the troll. "But the ticklish thing has spoiled my nighty-night time. I might as well go back out into the world and see what I can pillage." (Pillage is an old-fashioned way to say steal).

"You do that," said Princess Dania. "We'll work on our new song."

"A new song, hey?" The troll's voice brightened. "You can sing it for me tonight."

"Okay," Prince David and Princess Dania said together.

The troll's loud footsteps echoed through the hall once more, this time sounding farther and farther away until they could no longer be heard.

8

A Plan

Everyone piled out of the tunnel and gathered around the kittens' cage again.

Adelide sniffed Torrin's shoulder. "You smell like troll."

"At least I was brave enough to try to get the key," Torrin shot back. Fingers of doubt crept along his spine. He imagined travelling back to the palace to tell the king and queen they would never see their children again. He swallowed a lump in his throat.

Prince David and Princess Dania stared at them with sad eyes.

"Is there anything else you can think to try?" asked Prince David.

Jude clenched his hands at his sides. "Don't worry, we're not going to give up. There's six of us. I know we can think of something."

The children sat on the floor beside the cage, chins in their hands, except for Adelide, who paced back and forth through the troll's cavern, examining things on the shelves and rummaging through the contents of boxes and trunks.

Torrin's mind raced. *How can we get them out? We can't cut the bars. We can't get to the key.* He hung his head so low his chin dug into his chest. *It's hopeless.*

An idea pushed its way through the recesses of his mind. "Hey, does the troll ever let you out of the cage for any reason?"

Princess Dania nodded. "Yes, at night he gives us supper and then he lets us fly about the cavern to stretch our wings."

"Yes." Prince David wrinkled his nose. "And he makes us sing to him. We don't like that much."

"But he tethers us first." Princess Dania hid her eyes with her paws. "He makes us wear collars and chains so we can't fly very far."

"Oh, you poor dears!" Celeste's lips trembled.

"If only we could distract the troll somehow while you're out of the cage," said Jude. "Maybe we could create some kind of diversion."

"Too dangerous," said Torrin. "We don't know how fast he can run, and someone must free the kittens from the collars."

"True." Jude's shoulders sagged.

Adelide scurried back from the shelves. "What if we could get him to sleep while the kittens are still out of the cage?"

"How would we do that?" asked Jude. "Conk him over the head?"

"I would never suggest such violence!" Adelide showed them a jar. "See what I found on the shelf."

"Sleeping potion?" Celeste read. "But how would we get him to take it?"

Jude opened the jar, sniffed the contents, and made a sour face. "Yuck. This stuff smells terrible. Even if we could slip it into his water, he'd taste it immediately."

"Would milk mask the flavor?" asked David. "The troll loves milk, even more than we do."

"Maybe." Jude stood with his hands in his pockets, studying the shelves. "Where does he keep it?"

"He has a little hollow in the rocks back there." Dania gestured with her paw.

Torrin followed Jude. Sure enough, a shelf had been formed in one of the walls, with a thick cloth hanging across. The inside area was cool and damp.

"Here's a jar for milk." Jude held up a container. A few drops of milk coated the bottom. "This won't be enough to cover the taste of the sleeping potion."

"Maybe we can get some more." Torrin suggested. "Out in the village. Perhaps the troll won't notice that it's fuller."

"That's a big risk." Jude tapped the sides of the jar. "But I really don't think we have much of a choice."

They hurried back to the girls and the kittens.

Jude told them their plan. "The village is close and there are plenty of farmers, I'm sure. It shouldn't take us long to find a little milk."

"Are you sure this is a good idea?" asked Celeste.

"No, but I can't think of a better one." Torrin picked pieces of gravel left from the cave-in off the front of his shirt. "I mean, we've tried everything else and it almost got me eaten by a troll."

Celeste turned white. "Do you think the troll would have eaten you?"

Torrin instantly felt bad for scaring his sister. "I don't know, probably not. But he would have surely locked us in the cage, and then we'd have all been in trouble."

Jude pointed to the tunnel they'd come through. "You girls stay in there no matter what. Torrin and I will go get the milk."

"I beg your pardon." Adelide snapped. "Because we're girls, we can't come?"

"We-ell. We shouldn't all go," said Jude. "We might have to sneak into some place and four people aren't going to be able to do that very well."

"And someone should stay here with the kittens," said Celeste.

"Very well." Adelide waved her hand. "Jude, you should stay here with Celeste and the kittens. Torrin and I will search for the milk."

Torrin's tongue felt like a withered leaf. Going on a crazy mission with Jude was one thing. He trusted his brother more than anyone in the world. *But Adelide?*

Jude was nodding. "That makes sense. I should stay here with Celeste, in case the troll comes back. All right. You go with Torrin. But both of you be careful."

"We will," Torrin muttered. He agreed with the arrangement, but there was no reason to share this with Adelide.

"Hurry, hurry!" mewed the kittens.

Torrin rushed down the passage he hoped led to the outside world, with Adelide on his heels.

"What if we meet the troll on his way back?" Adelide huffed and puffed.

"It would be really bad," said Torrin. "But we can't think like that. We just have to hurry."

The passage was much wider and taller than the one they'd come through from the home of the gnomes. A few twists and turns, and they were out on a hillside, in the blazing sunshine.

As rushed as they were, it took a few minutes for Torrin's eyes to adjust to the sudden light. He staggered down the hillside, trying not to trip on the large boulders in the path.

"I hope this is the way to the village," said Adelide.

"There's no other road, so it has to be." Torrin shielded his eyes and looked out over the land. They could see for quite a distance. Cottages that seemed as small as doll houses dotted the hills. Creatures that appeared to be bugs, but must be cows and horses, grazed on green velvety hills.

Adelide and Torrin stared at each other.

"Cows," said Adelide.

"Milk!" exclaimed Torrin.

They slipped and slid down the mountain, paying no heed to bumps and bruises they gathered along the way.

After coming to a stop at the foot of the hill, Adelide brushed off her dress and began to run. Her cheeks were red, and her eyes sparkled. Torrin hadn't seen her so excited since she'd arrived at the palace.

He ran after her, and they zigzagged through the trees. A beaten path, undoubtedly created by the troll, continued through the forest.

Soon they came upon a slatted fence. Cows grazed in placid contentment across a wide, green field.

"Well, here we are," said Torrin. "I guess we stroll over and milk one?" He opened his satchel and pulled out the empty jar.

Adelide took the container and held it to the light. "I hope you're a good aim, because the top of this jar is pretty skinny."

Torrin groaned. "Why do you always have to be so gloomy? We'll figure it out."

Adelide put her hands on her hips. "Okay, Mister Know-everything. How many times have you milked a cow?"

"We-ell, never, but it can't be that hard, right?"

"I wouldn't know. I haven't tried either," replied Adelide.

"We'd better hurry. That troll could go back to the cave at any moment." Torrin climbed over the fence, hoping he appeared braver than he felt. *Are cows easily excitable? Are they . . . fierce?* He'd never thought about it before. He'd never even seen a cow up close, the milk in the palace was brought from the village.

A sturdy-looking black-and-white cow gazed at them with patient brown eyes.

It doesn't seem dangerous. Torrin stretched out his hand and approached it, trying to steady his trembling fingers. He hoped it wasn't like the palace watchdog, which pretended to be asleep until you were almost upon it, then exploded into a ball of frenzied barking and bared teeth. "So, where do we get the milk from?"

"Maybe ask it to let some down?" Adelide suggested.

"What are you doing!"

The voice came from the air, and almost caused Torrin to jump out of his skin. He leapt back and checked the sky.

Lester flew down and settled on the cow's back. "What are you children doing here? Your aunt has been worried sick about you all! Where are Jude and Celeste?"

Torrin pressed his hand to his chest and tried to gasp out an answer. "In–the cave still. We found–the kittens."

Lester's eyes widened. "Really? Well, that's great. Your aunt's been working with the gnomes to dig through the tunnel, since the treacherous mountain pass is impossible for anyone without wings to cross. Maggie sent me to search for you before she risked bringing the Windlesoar." He shifted to a less bony place on the cow's back. The animal continued to graze placidly.

"We need milk. That's why we came out here." Torrin gave Lester a hasty description of the plan.

"Let me get this straight . . . you came out here to get milk, but you've never been close to a cow?" Lester threw his little bat head back and roared with laughter. "And you–thought you could walk up and ask for some?"

Torrin's cheeks grew hot. "Hey, we're doing our best."

"Sorry. Whew. How about this idea?" Lester wiped his eyes with the corner of his wing. "Perhaps you could visit one of the nearby houses and ask a farmer?"

"Do you think they'll give us some?" asked Adelide.

"I don't know." Lester shrugged. "But you have a much better chance than getting it from a cow." He flapped back into the air. "Follow me!"

The children trudged through the field after him, trying to dodge piles of manure. Despite their efforts, their shoes were soon encrusted with goop.

Adelide held her nose. "I've decided I don't like cows."

"I thought royals were supposed to be tolerant," Torrin couldn't help but saying.

Adelide glared at him.

The farmer's house wasn't too far from the field. It sat in the open, like a fat, white chicken, with smaller buildings surrounding it. A wagon was parked outside.

"Good, looks like someone's home," said Lester.

Hens cackled in the yard as they approached, and a small scruffy dog bounded up, his entire body wagging along with his tail.

Torrin climbed the rough wooden steps and knocked on the door.

"Who's there?" came a woman's voice.

"Don't answer the door. It's probably that thieving old troll," answered a gruff man's voice.

"Please, we're not trolls," said Torrin.

"We're royals," said Adelide.

"You had to say it, didn't you?" Torrin rolled his eyes.

The door opened a tiny bit, just enough to see a peep of firelight.

"Oh, Charles, they are children." The woman pulled the door open further. She was about the same age as Torrin's queen mama. She wore a brown cap with a frilled edge and a blue dress with a crisp white apron. "Come in and let us know your business."

"Please, Ma'am, our feet are terribly muddy," said Adelide. "We would hate to dirty your nice clean floor."

"We don't have time to explain our mission." Torrin clasped his hands in front of him. "We came to beg of you, could you spare some milk? Our friends' freedom depends on it."

Lester landed on Torrin's shoulder, his claws digging into his shirt sleeve. "These children are with the Duchess Margarite. I trust you know who she is?"

A grizzled farmer, in long-john underwear and a battered hat, shuffled into the room. "Of course we know of the Duchess. Your friends wouldn't happen to have had a run-in with the infernal troll, have they?"

"Yes, Sir. Please, if we could have a little milk." Torrin said a silent, pleading prayer in his head.

"Oooh, Charley, we'd better help them," said the woman. "The Duchess Margarite is a wonderful soul who's helped many in trouble. The least we can do is help her."

"Yes," breathed Adelide. "Please hurry. We don't know when the troll will be back."

Torrin couldn't believe this was the same Adelide he had come to know. Her mouth turned down at the corners, and her voice warbled. *Is that a tear brimming in the corner of her eye?*

"All right, Sweetie," said the farmer's wife "We'll help you. No reason to cry." She turned in a flurry of her skirts and hurried to the other room

In a moment she was back with a new jar in her hands. "Fresh from this morning. Take it with our blessing."

"Maybe the Duchess Margarite could help us with our troll problem," grumbled the farmer as the children hurried to the door.

Torrin turned on his heel. "Have any of you thought about being his friend? Maybe he's lonely. Maybe if you asked nicely, he would give everything back."

The farmer rubbed his chin. "It's an unusual approach. I'll discuss it at the next town council meeting. Goodness knows we've tried everything else."

Torrin, Lester and Adelide rushed back the way they had come towards the cavern. The pleasant sun sent comforting beams to blanket their shoulders.

Torrin began to dread entering the dank damp cavern again, but it was unavoidable. *I must rescue my friends.*

At the entrance of the cave Lester paused, hovering in the air. "Let me go in first. If the troll has returned, I can escape easier than you can."

"Good idea," said Adelide. "You're quite thoughtful, for a bat."

"Thanks. I think," said Lester.

He flew into the dark cavern, his clicks ringing through the walls as he journeyed inside. In an instant, he was back. "All clear. But hurry."

Torrin and Adelide rushed through the cavern and into the troll's chamber. Everyone cheered as they set the bottle of milk on the table.

THE THREE ROYAL CHILDREN AND THE BATTY AUNT

Jude hastily consulted the packet of sleeping potion. "It says to mix in one spoonful. I'd better do two. The troll is awfully big."

Everyone held their breath as he measured the potion, capped the jar, and shook it. The milk had a slight tinge of purple, but otherwise appeared to be normal.

"I'll go put it back in the cold cellar," said Torrin. He grabbed the jar and headed to the little alcove where they'd found it.

Just as he was placing the jar on the shelf, the troll's voice boomed through the cavern. "Hello, my little friends! Did you miss me today?"

9

Rescue

Torrin yanked the cloth over the hole and dashed back into the lair. Everyone had already retreated to the tunnel. Jude's white face popped out for a second, then vanished.

Torrin scanned the room, his heart thudding. *Where can I hide? How can I get away?*

"The wardrobe! It's only half-full!" mewed David.

Torrin rushed to the coat closet beside the kitten's cage, jumped in among the coats and boots, and slammed the door shut. He peeped through the large keyhole. Sweat poured down his face.

The troll stomped into the room. In the brief time of his absence, Torrin had forgotten how large and frightening he was. *What will he do if he finds me?* He bit his lip. *He won't. He just won't. That's all there is to it.*

"Did you say something, my little pet?" The troll asked David.

"It's–nice to see you," said David.

"Did you have a good day?" asked Dania.

"Well, I found lots of goodies." The troll unslung a giant satchel from his shoulder. "I found a hat rack." He pulled out a shiny wooden specimen. "In case I steal any hats. I found a pitchfork, for if I steal any haybales." He reached all the way down and lifted out a giant round object, wrapped in burlap bags. Underneath was an enormous black caldron. When he pulled off the lid, steam curled from beneath it and the room was filled with a delicious scent. "Stew for our supper."

Torrin's mouth watered, and it seemed as though he'd eaten the cookies from the farmer's wife days ago, not hours.

"Give me a moment and I'll fetch your bowls," said the troll. "After my day in the nasty sun, I could go for a cold glass of milk." He rubbed his chin. "I can't remember if I have any left. Let me check."

He came back in a moment, carrying the bottle. "It's the strangest thing. I thought the milk was almost gone. Perhaps the fairies brought it to me."

The two kittens glanced at each other. "Maybe." Prince David gave a tiny smile.

"Ho, ho," said the troll. "Or my mind could be slipping. I've never seen fairies in these parts. Have you, kittens?"

"I don't think so," said Princess Dania

"No matter." The troll waved his hand. "However it got there, we'll have some now." he poured milk into two bowls, then snapped the cage door open. "Time to come out and play, friends."

"I wish I didn't have to chain you." He clipped chains to each of their leather collars. "But I can't have you flying away from me, can I?" He gave a surprisingly gentle chuckle.

Who does this troll think he is? You can't trap someone into being your friend. Torrin almost burst out of the wardrobe to give the troll a piece of his mind. Then he froze. *What if the kittens drink the milk?*

His fears were unfounded. The two kittens dipped their heads down as if to drink, but then allowed the liquid to dribble down their chins.

The troll, on the other hand, gulped the rest of the bottle down in a single swallow. The giant creature smacked his lips and stared down at the kittens. "Before dinner, why don't you sing me that same sweet song you sang to me yesterday?"

"The lullaby?" asked Dania.

"Yes, if that's what you call it," replied the troll.

Torrin grinned. *He's making this too easy.*

The two kittens closed their eyes, leaned against each other and began a sweet song.

"Perched on a ledge
Carved into a wall
Two little kittens,
In a royal hall
Resting on cushions,
With Mama to sing,
And bedtime stories
From Papa, the King,

Two little kittens,

Eyes heavy with sleep,

Soon off to dreamland,

To dance with the sheep.

Tears glittered on the kittens' cheeks.

They must miss their parents so much. Torrin's jaw clenched. *We have to get them home.*

The troll yawned and rested his head in his hands.

The kittens sang another verse, and another, a bit softer this time.

The troll's head nodded, and finally he slumped forward, his giant mouth open, booming snores issuing from the massive maw.

Torrin watched him for a moment to make sure he was actually asleep, then pushed open the wardrobe as quietly as he could. The kittens sat back on their haunches, their eyes never leaving the troll's face.

Torrin pulled out his dagger and examined their collars. They were too thick for his dull blade to tackle, and the buckles seemed complicated.

The chains connected to the kitten's collars had been fastened to a nail on the wall. Torrin unhooked them softly, catching the metal loops so they wouldn't clatter against the floor. He scooped up the kittens, and they perched on his shoulders, their soft wings brushing against his face.

As they crossed the room, a loop of chain caught on a chair-rail, and the chair crashed to the floor.

The troll stirred. "Wha-at?" His eyes flipped open.

Torrin ran, the kittens' tiny claws digging into his shoulders. Across the floor he went, finally popping into the cavern, where Jude, Adelide and Celeste waited.

"He's awake!" Torrin gasped. "Run!"

The troll's steps thudded across the room. His head filled the passage, and a long, skinny arm shot after them. But the grasping fingers could only come so far.

"He can't fit! Keep running!" yelled Celeste.

"Come back, friends!" the troll shouted. "Come–ba-a-a-ck . . ." his voice trailed away. Once again, loud snores filled the cavern.

A quick dash took the children to the area where the cave-in had occurred. "Now what?" Adelide put her hands on her hips. "We can't go through the wall and we can't get past the troll."

A rock bounced off the pile and landed at Torrin's feet. "watch out!" he yelped, jumping back.

More rocks bounced down and clattered among them.

"Everyone get back from the wall, it might be caving in worse!" shouted Jude.

"What will we do? What if we're trapped?" Tears poured down Celeste's cheeks.

The wall moved, and clouds of dust filled the cavern. Dirt filled Torrin's nose and he coughed and choked.

Adelide pointed to the rocks. "It's falling in!" she shouted.

The wall caved into itself, and a gaping hole was left behind.

Gnoom stepped out of the hole, blinking. "Hello, Children."

10

Return

Aunt Maggie rested her beautifully carved teacup on its saucer. "The moment I made it back through the passage I begged the gnomes to help me clear the rocks. This sort of thing happens to them from time to time, so they had special machines and stabilizers. They made short work of the rescue. But I was worried sick. I can't tell you how glad I was when Lester came back and informed me of your safety. And that you'd found the royal kittens!" She smiled at Princess Dania and Prince David, who were happily eating roasted trout provided by the gnomes.

"What do you think will happen to the troll?" asked Jude.

Gnoom set down a tray of cakes and folded his arms. "We'll be speaking to the residents of the town about him. In all the years he's been there he's stolen odds and ends, but never hurt or kidnapped anyone. The townspeople will have to overcome their cowardly ways and address the issue. The troll may be big, but he can't fight everyone."

"Maybe if they try to be his friend, he wouldn't act that way," said Adelide.

"Maybe." Gnoom nodded. "But he's going to have to learn that true friendship means giving to other people, not just taking what you want. Friendships cannot be forged when one person calls all the shots."

Adelide pursed her lips. "That's an interesting thought."

Aunt Maggie arranged her colorful shawl over her shoulders. "Children, Lester flew back to the Purrflyer kingdom as soon as you returned to the cavern. The entire royal army has probably been assembled to attempt their rescue. We must get these kittens back to their parents."

"Oh please, take us home," the kittens chorused.

Gnoom held up a thin, spindly finger. "Don't forget the reason you came to us in the first place."

He pulled a small object from his robe.

It was the sculpture of the kittens.

"Oh, it's beautiful!" Princess Dania gasped. "Mummy is going to love it!"

"I think she'll be happier to have you home." Celeste gave Princess Dania a tiny hug.

"Yeah." Prince David stared at the ground. "They're probably going to be pretty mad."

"I think they'll be too relieved to be angry," said Aunt Maggie. "Just wait and see."

As they ascended on the platform once more, they saw the king and queen waiting on the ledge of the cliff, just outside the castle.

"Oh, my darlings!" cried the queen. She stretched out her snowy white wings and flew to her babies, who were jumping up and down.

Prince David and Princess Dania cuddled with their mother, all of them purring so loudly Torrin could feel the vibrations from where he sat on the other side of the elevator.

"We got your birthday present, Mummy," said Princess Dania.

"And now, for honor and bravery shown at the most terrible time our kingdom has ever known, we shall bestow upon Duchess Margarite and the four royal children, the golden feather." The king proclaimed from his throne-platform.

Five matching calico cats with multi-colored wings flew to each person and hung thin golden chains, with golden feathers so fine they almost seemed real, around each of their necks.

Torrin's chest swelled with pride, but his heart thudded in relief. Every time he thought of the mean old troll he shuddered. "I'm glad we don't have to deal with trolls in our kingdom," he whispered to Adelide.

"My papa-king could handle him," she whispered back.

Torrin rolled his eyes. Adelide had been much nicer since they'd rescued the kittens, but every now and then her old annoying personality tiptoed back. He was learning to ignore it.

After a delicious feast of fried fish and creamy milk shakes, the children gave the Purrflyers hugs and climbed back on the platform to head home. The prince and princess tearfully promised to come and visit as soon as they could fly to other kingdoms.

"Or perhaps we can meet you halfway," Aunt Maggie said firmly. "It will be a few years before you're old enough to fly that far."

"Perhaps we will all fly together," said the Queen. "Good wishes, and a safe return home."

As the platform made its way down, Celeste asked, "Aunt Maggie, are all your adventures so dangerous?"

Aunt Maggie took her small hand and squeezed it in her large, wrinkled one. "Child, I have run from gryphons, snatched fox cubs from a giant's home, and flown just beyond the claws of dragons. But I would never have allowed you to go with me to that troll's lair if I'd have known the cavern was unsafe."

Torrin wrinkled his nose. "Well, I'm glad you didn't know. Everyone's okay, and we were able to save the kittens."

Aunt Maggie chuckled. "I'm not sure your parents will feel the same way."

A cold tremor surged through Torrin's soul. "What if Mama and Papa won't let us go on anymore adventures?" he whispered to Celeste.

"I heard that," said Aunt Maggie. "Never you mind about your parents. If they're worried, I'll just remind your mother of the time she crawled into a Moon-Mrat's nest to find a rare Homburn jewel. She still has it on a necklace, if I remember."

Torrin shook his head. It was hard to think of his parents out running about the world in crazy adventures. *They're just so . . . royal.* "It would be fun if Mama and Papa could come with us, just once."

"I wish I could go places with my papa," Adelide mumbled. "But he never takes me."

Celeste's mouth dropped open. "But . . . I thought you go with him everywhere."

Adelide put her face in her hands. "No. He thinks proper young ladies should stay at home and embroider and paint and learn manners. He only tells me stories about all the places he's visited and the people he's met. I changed them to be about me. I wanted you to like me. Your kingdom is the only place I've ever been besides my own."

Celeste patted her shoulder. "That's okay. Now you've been to the purrflyers kingdom too!"

Adelide brightened. "I have, haven't I? I bet my father's never even heard of the Gloming Gnomes!"

Aunt Maggie rubbed her chin. "I think I might have to pay a visit to your father, dear Adelide. Perhaps with help from the King and Queen, we can change his mind."

"Oh, would you please try?" A big, bright smile spread across Adelide's face. For the first time, she looked like who she was, a ten-year-old girl.

The platform landed with a thump.

"On to the Windlesoar!" said Aunt Maggie. "And then home!"

THE END

Did you enjoy *The Three Royal Children and the Batty Aunt*? You might like *The Amazing Adventures of Toby the Trilby*. Find it on Amazon!

https://amzn.to/2RJAL5a

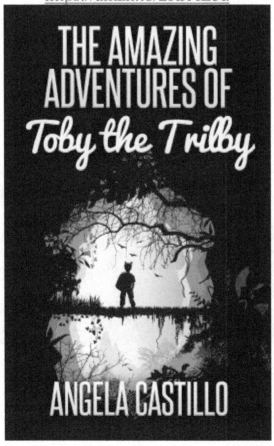

FAYETTE
— PRESS —

If you enjoyed *The Three Royal Children and the Batty Aunt*, you might also like these clean fantasy series (for teens and adults):

THE
SENTINEL TRILOGY

THE
STONES OF TERRENE

THE
UNDERWORLD MYTHOS

Blood-bonds with angels. Surreal mental abilities. Elemental gods. Maze Runner *meets* The Mortal Instruments *in this adrenaline-laced urban fantasy.*

Welcome to Terrene—where dragons exist, the past haunts, and magic is no myth. Welcome aboard the Sapphire.

Josh stumbled into the Underworld—rife with backstabbing fae and ancient powers—and he can't get out.

ABOUT THE AUTHOR

Angela Castillo loves living in the small town of
Bastrop Texas, and draws much of her writing inspiration
from life there. She loves to walk in the woods and
shop in the local stores. Castillo studied Practical Theology
and Music at Christ for the Nations in Dallas, Texas.
She was home-schooled all the way through high school and is the
oldest of seven kids. Castillo's greatest joys are her four children.

Made in the USA
Middletown, DE
22 April 2022

64625352R00070